Lukas and the Lion

A magical tale inspired by a child born
during the Covid–19 pandemic

By
David Gailey

Acknowledgments
This book would not have been possible without the advice and assistance of:
Catriona Hauser who encouraged me to complete the book and provided many suggestions to improve the evolving drafts.
Bob Harper who brought the story to life with the illustrations that were so necessary to complete the project.
Dawn Broadberry who turned a simple story into a published book.
Thank you to you all.
David

Lukas and the Lion

Published in Scotland by Dare BC Publishing
ISBN: 978-1-8382373-6-3 (paperback)
ISBN: 978-1-8382373-7-0 (ebook)

To my first grandson, Lukas.

May you enjoy the good health, wisdom and
many abilities the magic lion recognises in you.

Once upon a time …

…there was a wise prince and a wise and beautiful princess.

They met at a sorcerer's castle where they were taught mystical powers of how to turn people's silver into gold.

This meant that they could help the kings and queens of their lands make enough gold to feed and comfort their people.

They were much loved by the kings, queens and everyone in the land for their powers and wisdom.

They fell in love.

The princess married her prince in a castle in a far-off land where the prince lived.

People travelled from all around the world to celebrate their wondrous and joyful wedding.

They brought many gifts for the happy couple.

They partied long into the night.

Everybody was happy!

The next day the people felt sad when the prince and princess announced that they were going to live in an enchanted land, far, far away.

They were going to a land full of wonders and luxuries, where the sun always shone and where all things were possible.

While the people were pleased that such good fortune had come to the happy couple, they also felt sad that the enchanted land was so very far away, and it would not be easy to visit the prince and princess.

The enchanted land was ruled by a magical lion who looked after his people.

He wanted to make sure they were always safe and happy.

The lion gave the prince and princess three wishes.

He told them to use them wisely and guided them to take their time in making the wishes.

He said they should always think about who would benefit most from the wishes.

The prince and princess were truly happy in the enchanted land.

Soon they understood why the people at the wedding had shown such sadness.

The prince and princess missed the people from their own lands and knew that the people also missed the prince and princess.

They went to the lion to ask for their first wish.

They asked for magic mirrors so they could see and talk to the people and send pictures of their many adventures.

The prince and princess and the people were amazed at the marvellous magic mirrors they now owned.

Everybody was happy.

The prince and princess were so in love.

Every day in the enchanted land they discovered new wonders.

Together they would fly on winged dragons to nearby lands of mystery and beauty and return with pictures of their adventures to share in the magic mirrors.

One day, as they travelled home, they knew the time had come to have a child to share their enchanted world.

So they once again approached the magical lion.

They said that their second wish was to welcome a baby into the enchanted land.

The lion was pleased at their wise and thoughtful wish and told them to go back to their small, enchanted castle and prepare for the arrival of the child.

He asked them to think very carefully before using their third, and last, wish.

The prince and princess were pleased but knew that they lived in a small castle and that a larger castle was needed to welcome the baby.

Should they go to the lion and make this the third wish?

Wisely the prince and princess agreed that this would be a selfish wish of no benefit to anybody but themselves.

Instead they agreed to work hard and use their sorcery.

They turned more silver into gold for the lion and the kings and queens around the world, while saving enough gold to find a larger castle.

 The day arrived and the baby boy was born.

The prince and princess were overjoyed and showed him to the people in their own lands through the magic mirrors.

The people were most pleased and warmly welcomed the beautiful boy.

They exclaimed "Look as he smiles!"

"Look as he cries!"

"Look as he sleeps!"

The magic mirrors echoed "Look as, Look as."

The prince and princess said, "We shall name him Lukas in honour of the magic mirrors and of the joy he brings to the people in our lands."

As well as the joy they felt for Lukas, the people in their own lands shared an unhappiness.

A dangerous, evil spirit was roaming the lands.

People were hiding in their homes in fear of its wickedness, with only their magic mirrors to talk to each other.

Sadly, the prince and princess could not wish for the people to come to the enchanted land in case the evil spirit came with them.

The prince and princess went to the lion to talk
about the evil spirit and to wonder at the sadness
and fear it caused.

The lion explained that the evil spirit wished to enter
the enchanted land and he was using his magical
powers to keep the spirit away.

The lion knew his powers alone would not be
enough.

The lion could not keep the evil spirit away for long.

The prince and princess realised their third wish
could be used to help.

After many days and nights, caring for the new-born Lukas and wondering how best to use the third wish, they returned to the lion.

They said, "We wish for a magic potion to be given to every person in every land, not to destroy the evil spirit, but to keep each person safe from its powers."

The lion worked with the sorcerers in other lands to make enough magic potion to give to every person in every land.

While the sorcerers made the magic potion, the prince and princess turned more silver into gold to pay all the winged dragons to fly the magic potion to each person.

All around the world, each person received the magic potion and became safe from the evil spirit.

The evil spirit was now powerless against all the people of the world and so it wandered the lands, unable to do its evil.

A lonely and powerless spirit, hated by everybody now safe from it, slowly withered and died.

Free from the evil spirit, a sense of hope and long-lost inspiration filled the land, and the people could finally come out of their houses.

Lukas had only known life hiding from the evil spirit. But now his eyes lit up with wonder. Even at such a young age, he knew that something good had happened.

The prince and princess were happier than Lukas had ever seen. They were free to show him the wonders of the enchanted land and plan his first trip on a winged dragon to other lands.

In every land, the people rejoiced!

The people from the lands of the prince and princess were now free to go to the enchanted land to meet Lukas.

They all hugged and cried with joy when they were finally together.

The lion was proud of what he and the prince and princess had done.

To thank them he said, "As long as I live, I will watch over Lukas and make sure that he is safe."

He added, "I could grant Lukas good health, wisdom, and many abilities, but I know he has them already in abundance."

To all the children in every land he said, "Do not be afraid of evil spirits as we know now what to do. Stay home, stay safe with your magic mirrors, and wait for a magic potion to be delivered."

The End